Disney's

Little Library

Stories in this book

From James Hyams
18-3-86

Purnell

ISBN 0 361 06429 2

Copyright © 1984 Walt Disney Productions
Published 1984 by Purnell Books,
Paulton, Bristol BS18 5LQ,
Member of the BPCC Group
Made and printed in Great Britain by
Hazell Watson & Viney Limited,
Member of the BPCC Group,
Aylesbury, Bucks

Pinocchio

"This one has turned out very well!" exclaimed old Geppetto, putting the finishing touches to his wooden doll.

Afterwards he sighed and said:

"What a pity it is not a real boy! I would have so much liked to have a son!"

That night, as Geppetto was sleeping, the Blue Fairy appeared in the toymaker's shop. She touched the doll with her magic wand and immediately he came to life.

"Be a good boy and make Geppetto happy," said the fairy.

Geppetto was very happy and sent the boy to school. On the way, Pinocchio met two scoundrels who kidnapped him and sold him to a gypsy who had a theatre.

Stromboli, the gypsy, made him dance and sing on the stage, and Pinocchio earned a lot of money for him; but when the wooden doll said that he wanted to go home with his papa, he was shut up in a cage so that he could not escape.

Pinocchio cried bitterly until the Blue Fairy came to help him.

"How did you get here?" asked the fairy.

Pinocchio began to tell lies, and with each lie that he told his nose got a bit longer. Finally he said he was sorry, and the fairy freed him from his cage.

Unfortunately for our poor little friend, Pinocchio met the rascals again, who persuaded him into going to play in the 'Land of Toys'. He did not know that the two bad men only wanted to earn money at his expense.

In the 'Land of Toys' Pinocchio had a wonderful time, stuffing himself with sweets and ice-cream; and he also went on all the rides at a funfair and on which he could have as many turns as he wished.

However, that country was bewitched, and all the children who went there turned into donkeys. Pinocchio's ears and tail began to grow. Fortunately he was able to escape in time by throwing himself into the sea.

When he arrived home he found it deserted. Geppetto had gone out to look for him. A whale had swallowed the boat in which he had been travelling. Pinocchio felt ashamed when he thought that all this had happened because of him.

The little wooden boy threw himself into the sea to find the whale which had swallowed up his father. He managed to rescue Geppetto from inside the monster and together they swam towards the shore and safety.

The old man was not very strong and Pinocchio had to pull his father along as he swam. But the effort he made was so great that he lost his own life, although he managed to save Geppetto.

Geppetto wept and the fairy appeared.

"You have done well, my little friend," she said to Pinocchio. "I will change you into a real boy."

They were all very happy, and from then on Pinocchio was always a very good boy.

Snow White
and the Seven Dwarfs

The princess Snow White lived in the palace of her step-mother, where she worked and scrubbed and cleaned all the day.

The queen was a cruel witch who owned a magic mirror which she used to ask:

"Who is the most beautiful woman in the kingdom?"

"You, my Queen," the mirror used to reply.

Nevertheless, one day the mirror announced that the queen was no longer the most beautiful woman, but that it was Snow White. The step-mother,

furious, ordered that the princess should be taken to the middle of the wood, and then killed.

The man who was to kill her felt sorry for Snow White and spared her life. The little princess

was very frightened until a group of friendly
little animals took her to a little house in the
deepest part of the forest.

In the house lived seven nice dwarfs who welcomed the princess with great joy. They held a party to celebrate the arrival of their new friend, and everybody sang and danced.

The step-mother consulted her magic mirror and it told her that Snow White was living in the house of the dwarfs. The queen changed herself into an old hag and decided to kill the princess with a poisoned apple which she took with her.

"Be very careful and don't trust anyone,"
said the dwarfs, as they left the house. "It is
possible that the queen may try to harm you."

While she was alone, Snow White was
visited by the witch who asked her for something to drink.

"You are very kind," said the witch, pre-
tending to be friendly. "As a reward I will give
you the nicest apple in my basket."

When she bit into the poisoned apple, the princess fell to the ground as if she were dead. Just then the witch saw how the dwarfs were coming to help Snow White and fled to the mountains.

A terrible storm began and lightning killed the witch as a punishment for her wickedness. Afterwards the dwarfs picked up Snow White and carried her body to the wood.

An elegant prince came to the place where
the dwarfs were weeping beside their sweet
friend. Amazed at her beauty, he kissed her,
breaking the spell on the princess, who then
awoke instantly.

Soon afterwards the prince took Snow White back to his palace, to the great joy of the dwarfs. They married and lived happily ever after.

The Three Musketeers

Donald was very happy. It was his birthday and the postman had brought him an enormous parcel, a present from an unknown admirer.

"It has come from Brazil!" he exclaimed as he looked at the label. "What can there be inside?"

He tore the wrapping paper and was sur-
prised to find an enormous book, on whose
pages he could read 'This is Brazil'. But he was
truly amazed when the book opened suddenly
and a friendly creature appeared inside.

"My name is Jose Carioca," said the new arrival. "We have sent you this magic book so that you can learn about our country. Come along inside."

The pictures in the book were becoming real things, and soon the two of them found themselves walking in a city.

Carioca took Donald from one part of his beautiful land to another, telling him about all the wonderful things there. And so they visited Sao Paulo, part of the Amazonian jungle, and many other things.

"I would like to visit Rio de Janeiro," asked Donald. "I have heard so much about that city."

Very soon he found himself on the beach at Rio, surrounded by extremely beautiful girls in bathing costumes who welcomed him warmly, and even decorated him with flowers which they hung round his neck.

"Come on, my friend!" urged Carioca. "There is still the Carnival."

"This is something!" yelled Donald excitedly. "The carnival of Rio, the most famous in the world! Let's go and dance!" And in fact, very soon afterwards, our friend the duck was dancing the well-known Samba played by Bertie Blewitt and his Banjo Boys.

But the excitement was not over yet for Donald. Suddenly there was a deafening fanfare of trumpets and tremendous explosions, and a friendly cockerel dressed as a Mexican appeared in front of them.

"I am Panchito," he declared, as he put his revolvers back in their holsters. "I have come to invite you to visit my country. You are going to see something really special, my twin brothers!"

He took them to a little village where they were celebrating, and Carioca, Panchito and Donald sang beautiful Mexican love-songs.

Afterwards, they climbed onto Panchito's
blanket, which rose into the air as if it were a
magic carpet, and they were able to visit
several towns, each one more beautiful and
interesting than the last, while their friend told
them all about their history.

Mexico City was also celebrating and Donald was lucky enough to join in. They blind-folded him and he tried to break a 'pinata', a jar full of sweets, which was very difficult because every time he was about to hit it, his friends pulled it away on a rope.

Panchito demonstrated his skill at bull-fighting, although on this occasion it was not a real bull, but a dummy head with rockets shooting from its horns, which exploded noisily. It was very exciting.

Once the fiesta was over they went back to
Donald's house. The three new friends
embraced each other affectionately, promising
to meet again.

They went so far as to make up a song which
was, "We are the Three Musketeers, we all go
after the first oooooooooone!"

The Flying Donkey

L ittle Gaucho had come out of his house very early intending to hunt a condor.

After climbing up the mountain for a long time, he sat down to rest for a moment. It was then that he saw a nest with enormous wings sticking out of it on a far-away peak.

"It must be the biggest condor in all the Andes!" he exclaimed. "And by the size of the wings I will have a new world record."

He got his bolas ready to hunt, but they fell from his hands when he saw a little donkey with wings appear out of the nest.

The little donkey began to fly as if it was a
bird. Little Gaucho recovered from his surprise
and threw his bolas at it entangling its legs; but
the flying donkey slipped easily out of the cord
and dive-bombed at the little boy, knocking
him over onto his back.

"This little animal wants to play," said Little Gaucho, "but it's much too valuable an animal to allow it to escape. I must catch it."

Several times he tried to capture it, but the little donkey escaped him easily, knocking over the little boy to send him sprawling on the ground.

Since it was impossible for him to catch the little flying donkey, Little Gaucho began to go away regretting his bad luck. But the little flying donkey followed him quietly, trying to show him that he wished to be his friend.

Little Gaucho spent several days taming him.

Soon Little Gaucho was able to ride the flying donkey. It was splendid to fly on the back of such a wonderful animal.

One day, Little Gaucho saw a poster advertising horse-racing, which was to take place in a nearby town.

On the day of the race, Little Gaucho turned up riding on his little donkey. He had hidden his mount's wings underneath a blanket, and all the big gauchos laughed loudly when they saw him.

"This titch, on his donkey, wants to race against the best horses!" they said.

"He who laughs last laughs best!" replied Little Gaucho.

The gauchos, who had not stopped mocking the little boy, lined up, waiting for the marshal to start the race.

"Now!" he yelled. And all the horses set off at a gallop.

The flying donkey was very frightened and began to buck, almost throwing his rider, who hung on tight to the neck of his mount, making the crowd laugh. Once he had got over his fright the little donkey set off after the horses at a gentle trot.

When no one could see them, Little Gaucho dismounted and set about taking off the blanket which covered the wings of the wonderful donkey.

"Now to show those gauchos what running is," said Little Gaucho as he got on again. "Let's go, little donkey."

Little donkey set off like the wind, flying
very low, and soon caught up with the rest of
the horses, which he passed in a flash. The
gauchoes could not see the donkey's wings as
he was going too fast, but they were amazed.

Little Gaucho crossed the finishing line well ahead of the other runners.

"He cheated!" shouted everybody.

And Little Gaucho had to fly away on his donkey to escape the angry judges.

The Ice-cold Penguin

We all know that penguins live in the frozen wastes of the South Pole and that they are happy, despite the intense cold.

This is the story of Percy, the only penguin in the world who was not happy, because he was always, always cold.

Percy hardly ever left his house. He stayed beside his beloved stove, and when he did go out it was to take a hot bath in his bath-tub.

One day, tired of suffering from the cold, he decided to emigrate to warmer lands.

The truth is that Percy did not get very far.
He could only manage a few steps.
Immediately he began to feel that his feet and
beak were freezing and that he was quite ill.
His fellow penguins found him half-frozen and
they had to rush him back to the stove.

When he was better, he began to think about how to get to a warmer country.

"I know what I will do!" he said happily to himself.

He wrapped himself up in hot-water bottles, which he tied round his waist, with a thick woollen overcoat on top, and he set off again.

This time he felt fine. But when he stopped a few moments to consult his maps the heat from the hot-water bottles melted the ice underneath his feet and he sank into the frozen waters of the Arctic.

His friends took him home again.

This further set-back really put him off trying to get away. So he spent several days looking with jealous eyes at the posters from sunny parts of the world which he had on his walls. There was one on which he could see a splendid boat glowing in the sunlight.

"Why didn't I think of that before!" he said to himself, hitting his forehead. "That's what I need—a boat!"

From that moment he began to be terribly busy. He fixed a post in front of his house, to which he fastened a sail; he cut the ice round about . . . and he had a boat!

For days and days the little ice boat sailed to the north without changing course. From time to time Percy looked at his maps so as not to go the wrong way.

"If I go on like this, in a few days I will reach the South Sea Islands of my dreams."

And so it was. As he got further north, the
sun got warmer and Percy ventured out of his
ice house to lie in the sun and warm himself.
But of course, as well as warming him, it also
warmed the ice boat.

One day, when the sun was very warm, Percy noticed anxiously that his ice boat was melting too quickly. With a tremendous SPLASH! the stove slid into the sea and the penguin had to seek safety in the bath-tub.

But the water came through the plug-hole!

"I have a good idea!" exclaimed Percy as he put the shower head into the plug-hole of the bath-tub. "If the water comes out of the shower-head it will push me along as if it was a motor."

And so, quite soon, he sailed towards a nearby island.

When he reached the tropical island, Percy
began to jump up and down for joy. He
immediately hung a hammock and lay in it to
sunbathe.

Now, very brown, I think that as he fans
himself to keep cool, occasionally he longs for
the coolness of the frozen regions of the Pole.